D0596690

YODA'S MISSION

Written by Emeli Juhlin

Based on the episode "Yoda's Mission,"
by Lamont Magee and Michael Olson

PRESS

LOS ANGELES • NEW YORK

This is Nubs.
Nubs is training to
become a Jedi Knight.
Jedi use lightsabers.
A lightsaber is a laser sword.
Nubs and his friends
are trying to finish
a training course.

When Nubs is almost to the
finish line, he nearly falls!
Nubs needs help
from his friend Kai.

Kai drops his lightsaber.
Kai has to choose to get
his lightsaber or to help Nubs.

Kai cannot do both.
He chooses his lightsaber.
They do not finish the course.
Kai tells Nubs he is sorry.

Yoda visits the younglings.

He saw Kai choose his lightsaber.

He tells Kai to help others.

Lightsabers can be replaced.

Yoda has a special mission
for the younglings.
He needs a secret item.

The item is for a special event.
Yoda gives them instructions.
They leave on their mission.

Taborr and his pirate crew spy on the younglings. They want to steal the secret item.

Nash, RJ-83, and the younglings
follow Yoda's instructions.
The secret item is seeds!

Before they head home,
they receive a distress signal.
Someone needs help!

They follow the signal.

It is Taborr!

Taborr tricked them.

He stole the seeds.

Kai, Lys, and Nubs
borrow Nash's speeder.

They have to find Taborr
and get the seeds back.

The younglings sneak
onto Taborr's ship.
They find the seeds.
Nubs makes a loud noise.

The pirates hear the noise.
They come to stop the younglings.

Kai distracts Taborr.

Lys and Nubs escape.

When Nubs tries to
jump onto Nash's ship,
he nearly falls!
Nubs needs help from Kai again.

Taborr takes Kai's lightsaber!
Kai has to choose to get
his lightsaber or to help Nubs.

Kai makes the right choice.

He uses the Force to help Nubs.

The Force is a magical energy field.

Kai saves Nubs!

Nubs thanks Kai for helping him.

The younglings get back
just in time for the
special ceremony.

The younglings give the seeds
to Master Yoda.
They are rare sparklefire seeds.

When planted, the seeds
turn into beautiful flowers.

They are a symbol of friendship between the Jedi and the people of the galaxy.

Kai tells Yoda he lost
his lightsaber on the mission.
Yoda is proud of Kai.

Kai chose to help others.
Yoda gives Kai the lightsaber
he used when he was a youngling.

he will be a
great Jedi someday.

Just like the sparklefire seeds,
the younglings will grow up
strong and bright.